I Sing for the Animals

From out of the earth
I sing for the animals;
I sing for them.

Red Streaked Around the Face
Hunkpapa Sioux

I Sing for the Animals

by Paul Goble

Bradbury Press   New York

Collier Macmillan Canada   Toronto

Maxwell Macmillan International Publishing Group
New York   Oxford   Singapore   Sydney

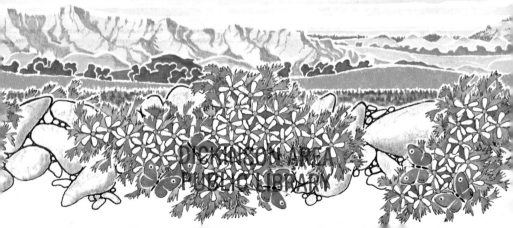

For Janet and Robert, with love

Bradbury Press
Macmillan Publishing Company
866 Third Avenue
New York, NY 10022

Collier Macmillan Canada, Inc.
1200 Eglinton Avenue East
Suite 200
Don Mills, Ontario M3C 3N1

Printed in the United States of America
    2   3   4   5   6   7   8   9   10

The full-color illustrations have been reproduced from the original
artwork. They frame sections of the paintings Paul Goble has done
for his celebrated books about the Plains Indians: *The Gift of the
Sacred Dog, Star Boy, The Great Race, Her Seven Brothers, Beyond
the Ridge,* and *Dream Wolf.*

Library of Congress Cataloging-in-Publication Data
Goble, Paul.
    I sing for the animals / written and illustrated by Paul Goble. —
1st ed.
        p   cm.
    Summary: Reflects on how we are all connected to everything in
nature and how all things in nature relate to their Creator.
    ISBN 0-02-737725-3
    1. Nature—Religious aspects—Juvenile literature. 2. Creation—
Juvenile literature. [1. Creation. 2. God.] I. Title.
BL435.G62   1991
242'.62—dc20   90-19812

85067

The thoughts in this small book are not Native American, although I am undoubtedly influenced by the lifelong association. I have been helped by rereading letters from the 1950s, written to me when I was in my teens and living in England, by Father Gall Schuon of the Abbaye Notre-Dame de Scourmont in Belgium. Other influences may be my Quaker forebears and Church of England schooling. In the main, these are some of the thoughts which have come during thirteen years away from "civilization" in the silence and beauty of the pine tree forests, living with the seasons, the wild birds and animals, plants, and insects.

This book is for children and grown-ups who love wild flowers and grasses more than mowed lawns; who cry for the birds and animals killed for "sport" or "necessity" and imprisoned in zoos and cages. It is for all who guard, and champion, Father Sky and Mother Earth.

THE EARTH IS THE LORD'S, AND THE FULLNESS THEREOF; THE WORLD, AND THEY THAT DWELL THEREIN.

A LL things in nature reflect their Creator. Everything tells us something about God.

THE birth of each new day is a sacred ceremony: the earth awakes, refreshed from the night. First one bird starts to sing, and one by one they all join in chorus. The sky brightens, changing from white to pink to blue, and then the sun comes up with golden light.

PLANTS and trees, birds and animals, all things like us to talk to them. They want to speak to us, too, but it is not easy for them. We have to find a way to understand what they are saying to us.

WE see God in the sun and the moon, and in rocks and mountains, and in all the works of his Creation. We draw near to him when we are close to the things which he has made.

WE are thankful to be alive. Everything wants to live. Hawks and eagles kill so they can eat. It is the same with wolves and weasels. The Creator intended it to be that way; it reminds us that one day we, too, will die.

W E are related to everything
in nature. We share the
earth with all our relatives.

WE need not feel lonely in the fields and woods. Birds and animals, and the butterflies, speak to us. Often we are not really looking or listening. It is the same at night: the stars speak to us. We have to learn to look, and to listen. We are never alone.

G OD made man and woman
after making everything else.
Because the birds and animals, the
weeds and grasses, the fishes and
insects, are so much older than us,
we respect them

BIRDS pray, trees pray, flowers pray, mountains pray, the winds and rain pray, rivers and the little insects as well. We hear them. The whole earth is a constant prayer, and we can join with this great prayer.

NOTHING in nature is evil. We may sometimes dislike flies or spiders, the skunk or snakes, and yet they only do what their Creator means them to do.

G OD'S voice is the silence
of the sky, the great open
plains, and the high mountaintops.
We hear him speaking to us like
silently falling snow.

MAN'S world changes, and we hardly feel at home in the places where we grew up. The natural world is constant: the sun comes up and goes down, and the seasons follow one another and return again like a great circle. Flowers and trees give birth to the same colors and shapes year by year. Buttes and rocks seem to remain forever unchanged. In our own changing world, it is these things which give us strength and stability.

EVERYTHING is tired at the end of the day. We are tired, too.
Darkness and silence come.
We sleep, and are made pure and new again during the night.

O LORD, HOW MANIFOLD ARE THY WORKS!
IN WISDOM HAST THOU MADE THEM ALL;
THE EARTH IS FULL OF THY RICHES.